# A Wild Ride in Texas

Reader's Digest Young Families

Senior Designer: Elaine Lopez
Editor: Sharon Fass Yates
Editorial Director: Pamela Pia

Published by Reader's Digest Young Families, an imprint of The Reader's Digest Association, Inc.
Reader's Digest Road, Pleasantville, NY U.S.A. 10570-7000
Written by Christina Wilsdon copyright © 2006 Reader's Digest Young Families.
Illustrations by Susan Jaekel copyright © 2006 Reader's Digest Young Families.
Page 27: Mockingbird copyright © 1982 Reader's Digest Association, Inc. Texas map and Bluebonnet copyright © 1992 Reader's Digest Association, Inc. Background map copyright © 2005 Map Resources.

All rights reserved. No part of this publication may be reproduced or utilized in any form or by any means, electronic or mechanical, including photocopying, recording, or by any information storage or retrieval system, without written permission from the Publisher.

The Read and Write with the Country Mouse and the City Mouse logo and Reader's Digest Young Families are trademarks of The Reader's Digest Association, Inc.

Library of Congress Cataloging-in-Publication Data

A wild ride in Texas / written by Christina Wilsdon; illustrated by Susan Jaekel.
p. cm. -- (Read and write with the country mouse and the city mouse)
Summary: When Emma the country mouse, and Henry the city mouse go to the Texas State Fair to enter Emma's macaroni and cheese recipe in the cooking competition, they learn a lot about America's second biggest state.
ISBN-13: 978-1-59939-011-6 (hardcover)
ISBN-10: 1-59939-011-6 (hardcover)
(1. Fairs--Fiction. 2. Mice--Fiction. 3. Animals--Fiction. 4. Texas--Fiction.) I. Jaekel, Susan M., ill. II. Title.
PZ7.W68577Wil 2006
(E)
(2

2005031225

Printed in China.

10 9 8 7 6 5 4 3 2 1

# A Wild Ride in Texas

Written by
Christina Wilsdon

Illustrated by
Susan Jaekel

Reader's Digest Young Families

"Look! Oil rigs!" shouted Emma, pointing out the window of the airplane as she and her cousin Henry flew above the coast of Texas.

"Those oil rigs are in the Gulf of Mexico," said Henry. "The airport isn't far from here. We'll be landing soon!"

"I can't wait to get to the Texas State Fair," said Emma. "I'm eager to see how a little ole' country mouse's macaroni-and-cheese recipe will do in the cooking competition!"

Soon their little plane was bumping along a runway. Then it slowed to a stop. Henry and Emma took their bags and climbed down the steps of the plane.

"Henry! Emma! Over here!" called a voice. The two mice looked around quickly, then spotted the owner of the voice—an armadillo wearing a cowboy hat.

"Howdy, you two!" cried the armadillo. She grabbed Henry's hand and gave it a firm shake, then swept Emma up in a hug. "Welcome to Texas!"

"Good to see you, Amy!" said Henry. "I'd recognize you anywhere!"

"Boy, are we going to have fun," said Amy. "But before you take another step, I'm going to get you looking a little bit more Texan."

With that, she plopped a cowboy hat on Henry's head and another on Emma's.

"Is this what you call a ten-gallon hat?" asked Emma.

"You can call it that if you like," said Amy, "but Emma, you'd be swallowed up whole by a ten-gallon hat. Why, you could live in a ten-gallon hat! This here's what I'd call a quarter-pint hat."

Amy led the two mice to her truck. They hopped in and zoomed away from the airport.

"I live on a ranch," said Amy. "My next-door neighbors are longhorn steers. Well, actually, since I live in a hole in the ground, I guess they'd be my upstairs neighbors!"

"I'll feel right at home," said Emma. "I often see cows strolling by my house in the countryside where I live."

"If the steers stomp their feet, I'll feel at home, too!" added Henry. "Sometimes I think there are buffalo living in the apartment above mine in the city!"

The land was flat as a pancake for miles around. A cloud of dust whirled behind their little car as they bumped across the dirt and zipped past a steer. They finally stopped by a sign that said "Amy's Ranch."

"Everybody out!" hollered Amy.

That evening, Henry and Emma relaxed outside the burrow while Amy prepared dinner.

"Chili?" asked Amy as she popped up out of the ground.

"No," said Emma. "I'm not a bit chilly. I feel just fine, thanks."

"Not that kind of chilly," said Amy, giggling. "I mean red-hot chili! Piping hot, spicy beans and lots more!"

"Oh!" said Emma. "Silly me. Why, yes, please."

Amy ladled chili onto two plates and gave them to Henry and Emma. The two mice eagerly tasted their meal. Then Henry's face turned red. Emma's eyes popped.

"Wow!" said Henry. "This chili is hot stuff."

"Oh, dear," said Amy. "I tried to tone it down and make it not too hot. My usual chili recipe is so spicy, it would shake the rattles off a rattlesnake and make steam come out of your ears. I'm going to enter it in the big state fair this month!"

"Very tasty," said Emma. She quickly gulped down a glass of water.

The next morning, Emma and Henry watched Amy get her small airplane ready for their trip to the fair.

"We'll take off in just a few minutes," said Amy. "We're going to take a roundabout route to Dallas so you can see a little more of the second-biggest state in the USA!"

Suddenly a big wiry brown ball bounced into view. It rolled gently to a stop in front of Emma.

"What's this?" asked Emma, touching it gently.

"I do believe that's a tumbleweed plant," said Henry.

Emma held it with both hands and lifted it. "Why, it's so light," she said.

Just then a breeze blew by. It picked up the tumbleweed and sent it rolling and bouncing across the ground—with Emma attached!

"Help!" cried Emma.

"Emma!" cried Henry.

"Oh, no!" cried Amy.

Suddenly the ground began to shake beneath Henry and Amy's feet. A big shadow fell over them.

"Looks like you could use some help," said a deep voice.

Henry looked up—and saw that the speaker was a pony.

"Dusty, you're in the nick of time," said Amy. "We've got to chase down that tumbleweed and rescue Emma."

"Hop aboard!" said Dusty. He lowered his nose to the ground. Henry and Amy took hold of his mane and climbed up onto his back.

"Giddyap!" cried Amy. Dusty bolted forward and galloped across the field.

Soon they caught up with the runaway tumbleweed. Emma was inside the middle of the round weed, clinging tightly to its branches. Dusty grabbed the top of the tumbleweed in his teeth to stop it.

Emma jumped down to the ground. "Thank you so much for rescuing me! I was beginning to get dizzy from all the tumbles this tumbleweed was giving me!" said Emma.

After Henry and Emma were seated in the plane, Amy shouted from the pilot's seat, "Buckle up. Here we go!"

The plane soared into the air. Henry and Emma gazed down at the land below that stretched on and on and on.

"Let's see, it's ten o'clock now," said Amy. "We should be at Big Bend National Park by early evening."

"Excuse me," said Emma. "Did you say evening?"

"I sure did," said Amy. "There are a whole lot of miles between us and the park! If we flew past the park into the western tip of Texas, we'd be in a whole other time zone!"

Miles of sagebrush plants rolled by as they flew west. Finally the plane touched down in the park. The three travelers quickly set up camp. Then they roasted marshmallows as they watched the sunset.

Henry, Emma, and Amy spent the next few days exploring the park. Every night, Emma tried out a new macaroni-and-cheese recipe for dinner. Henry and Amy pretended to be judges.

One morning, Henry yawned and stretched as he stepped out of his tent. Then *plop!* He fell into a shallow hole in the ground.

"Where did this pit come from?" he asked. "It wasn't there last night."

Amy took a look. Her eyes grew wide. "That's a cat footprint," she said.

"A cat footprint?" Emma gasped. "Why, it's longer than I am! I know you said everything is bigger in Texas, but—even your cats?"

Amy laughed. "I didn't mean a kitty-cat," she said. "When I say cat, I mean mountain lion! We're lucky it didn't stop to take a closer look!"

"Could it be hiding nearby?" asked Henry nervously.

They quickly packed up their gear and took off in the plane before they could find out the answer!

"We're just about halfway to Dallas," announced Amy later that day as they descended for a landing. "We're going to stop here in Abilene and take in a rodeo."

"You mean bucking broncos and bulls?" asked Henry. "Roping steers and barrel racing?"

"Those events are not for us," replied Amy. "We critters have our own rodeo."

Soon the three travelers were at the rodeo grounds. They ducked into a tent filled with mice, armadillos, and other animals, waving their hats and cheering.

Henry read the program. "They have jackrabbit jumping!" he exclaimed. "It says, 'See if you can stay on a bucking bunny for at least eight seconds without being bounced off!' I'm willing to give that a try!"

He signed up for the event, then drew a name from a hat. "Hopalong Rabbit," read Henry out loud.

"That's him, over there!" said Emma, pointing to a big jackrabbit dozing in a pen.

"Go say howdy to him," suggested Amy.

Henry climbed up the side of the jackrabbit's pen. "Howdy!" he called.

The jackrabbit opened an eye and wiggled an ear. "Well, howdy!" he replied with a smile. "Are you my lucky rider? I promise I won't bounce you too hard!"

"See that you don't!" Henry laughed. He jumped aboard the jackrabbit and held tightly to his fur.

"And now, up next," the announcer shouted, "Henry the city mouse aboard Hopalong Rabbit!"

Hopalong burst out of the pen. He bounded high into the air, kicked once, and off Henry sailed. *Poof!* Henry landed in a soft pile of sand.

"Good try," said Hopalong. "You lasted two seconds. Not bad for a tenderfoot! In Texas, that's what we call a beginner."

The next day, Henry, Emma, and Amy arrived in Dallas. They landed just outside the fairgrounds.

"Here we are," said Amy. "This is the biggest state fair in the country. It has been held every year for over one hundred years!"

"Welcome!" boomed a voice that came from a giant cowboy statue looming over them. Henry, Emma, and Amy had to lean way back to see the top of the statue.

"That looks like a fifty-gallon hat on his head!" said Henry.

"You're close!" said Amy. "It's seventy-five gallons!"

The fair was a whirlwind of excitement. Henry tried cotton candy for the first time—in five different colors! Emma tried her luck at throwing a spongy cheese ball into buckets and won a prize—a stuffed toy cactus that was bigger than she was!

"Let's take a look at the program," said Emma. "I need to take a break so I can make my macaroni-and-cheese dish in time for the food competition."

"Okay," said Henry. "That's in the tent over there."

"That must be where the chili contest is, too," said Amy. "I've also got to get cooking. I'm going to make the best 'bowl of red' those judges ever tasted!"

While Amy and Emma cooked, Henry took a stroll through the exhibition tents. He examined farming tools, tractors, and quilts. There was even a display of statues carved out of butter!

Later, when he came back to the cooking tent, Henry spied a big blue ribbon on Emma's macaroni-and-cheese dish and another on Amy's chili! "First prize!" he cried. Amy and Emma beamed proudly.

"Thanks to Amy's secret chili sauce," said Emma. "I added some to my mac-and-cheese to give it a little zing!"

"And the rest of the bottle went into my chili," said Amy.

"And now it's time to try out the rides," said Emma. "Let's start with the Ferris wheel, so we can get a good look at them all!"

"It's one of the biggest in the United States," noted Amy.

"Of course," said Henry, winking. "Everything's bigger in Texas!"